INTO THE UNDER WORLD

GILLIAN CLEMENTS

WALKER BOOKS
AND SUBSIDIARIES
LONDON · BOSTON · SYDNEY

This is your new home. Imagine running about inside, upstairs and downstairs! When you descend into the deep, dark cellar, imagine you find a trapdoor. You lift it to reveal a tunnel! And now imagine that you are sliding

down ...

down ...

down...

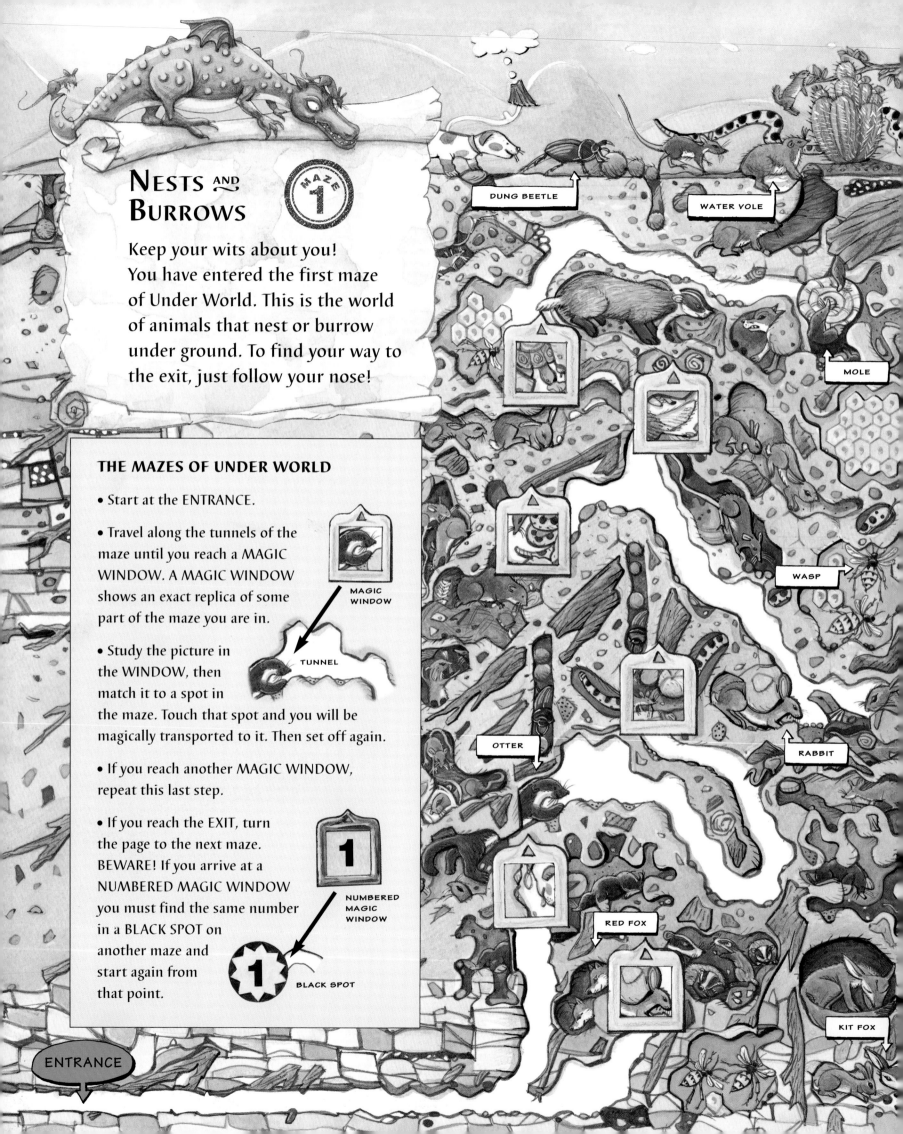

NESTS AND BURROWS

Keep your wits about you! You have entered the first maze of Under World. This is the world of animals that nest or burrow under ground. To find your way to the exit, just follow your nose!

THE MAZES OF UNDER WORLD

• Start at the ENTRANCE.

• Travel along the tunnels of the maze until you reach a MAGIC WINDOW. A MAGIC WINDOW shows an exact replica of some part of the maze you are in.

MAGIC WINDOW

TUNNEL

• Study the picture in the WINDOW, then match it to a spot in the maze. Touch that spot and you will be magically transported to it. Then set off again.

• If you reach another MAGIC WINDOW, repeat this last step.

• If you reach the EXIT, turn the page to the next maze. BEWARE! If you arrive at a NUMBERED MAGIC WINDOW you must find the same number in a BLACK SPOT on another maze and start again from that point.

1

NUMBERED MAGIC WINDOW

1

BLACK SPOT

DUNG BEETLE

WATER VOLE

MOLE

WASP

RABBIT

OTTER

RED FOX

KIT FOX

ENTRANCE

BURIAL CHAMBERS

MAZE 3

Beware the mummy's curse! Beware the spooks! Beware the Numbered Magic Window! Is there a ghost of a chance that you can negotiate the crypts and catacombs of the third maze?

CURIOUS COFFINS

CRYPT

GRAVE ROBBERS

ANGLO-SAXON GRAVE

ENTRANCE

EGYPTIAN TOMB

CHARIOT GRAVE

BEWARE THE BLACK DEATH

BRONZE AGE BARROW

MAYAN TOMB

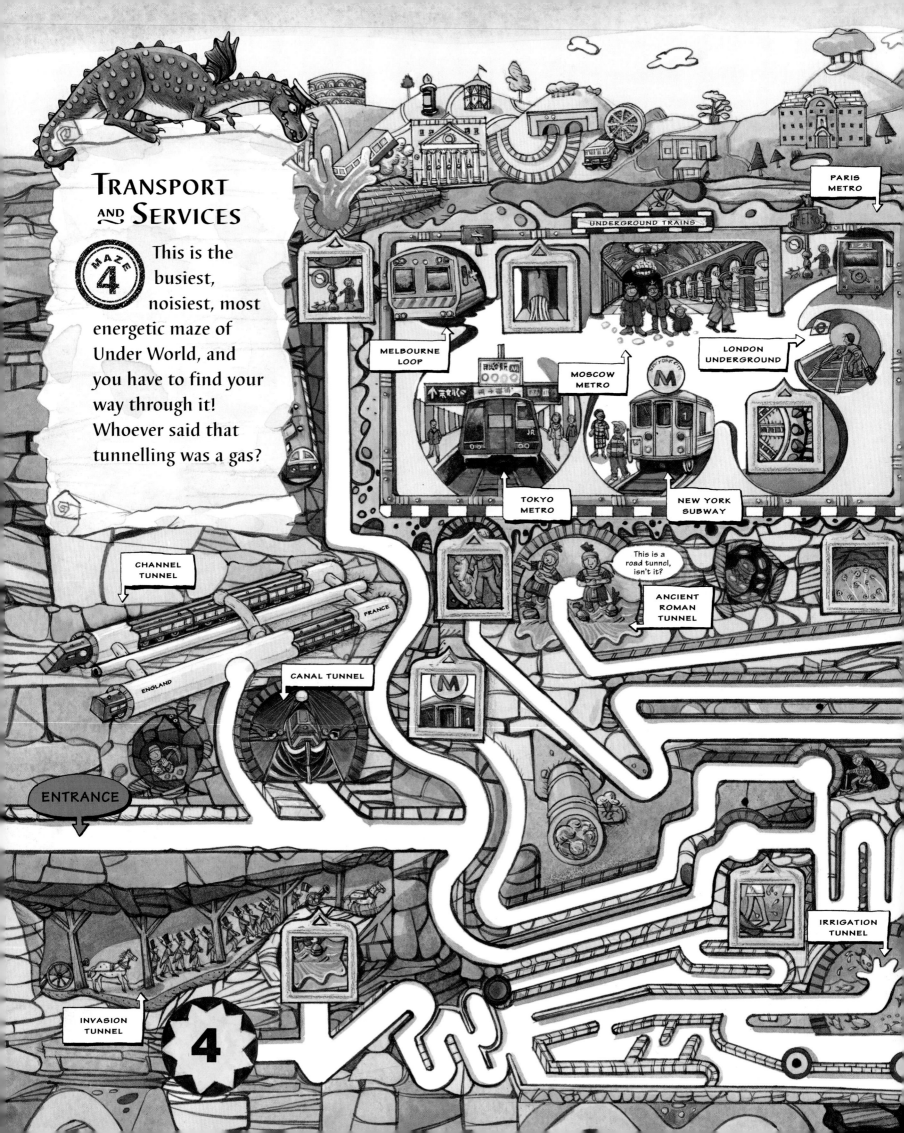

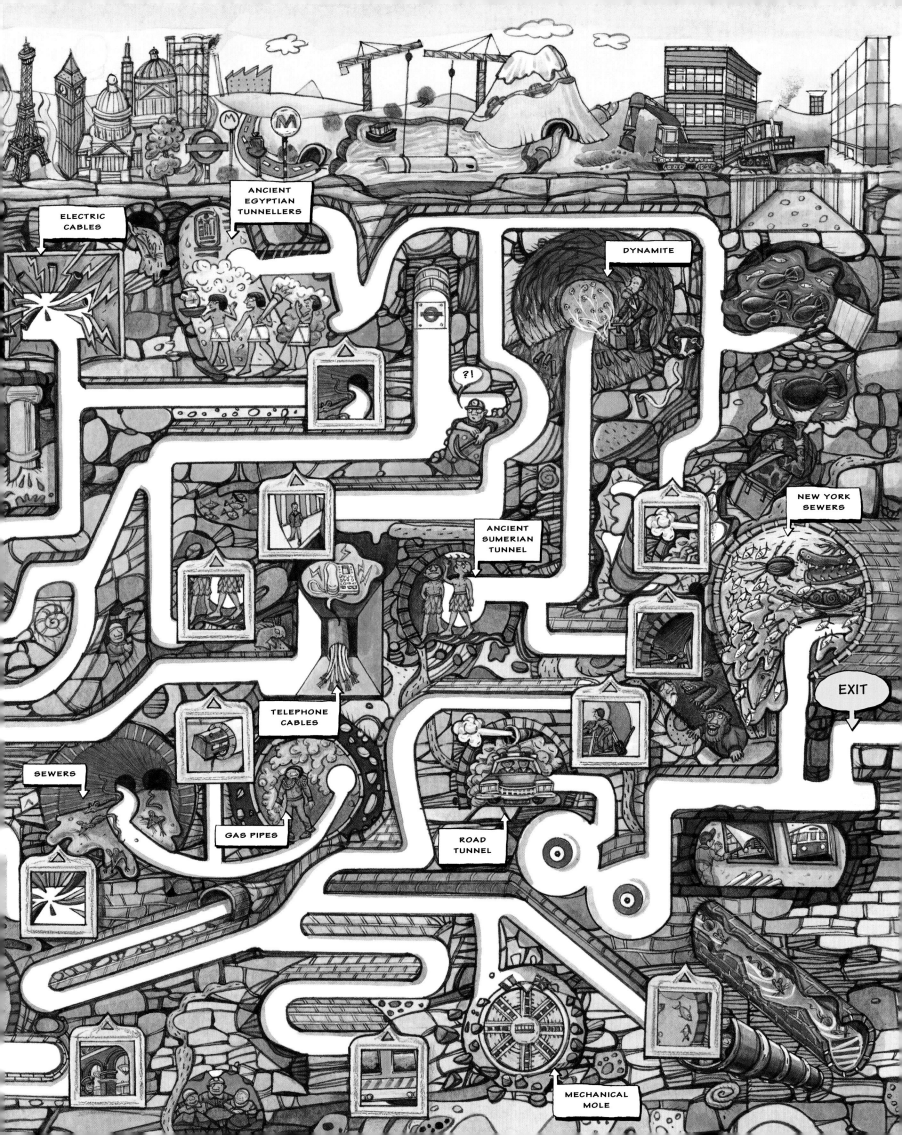

MYTHS AND STORIES

MAZE 6

Beware the fearsome Minotaur! Beware the monsters of myth. Beware the Numbered Magic Window! Blaze a trail through the most mysterious maze of Under World.

TO ATLANTIS

ALI BABA

TEUTONIC DWARFS

GATE OF DEMONS

GOBLINS

MINOTAUR

ALADDIN

BEOWULF

COUNT DRACULA

ENTRANCE

KING SOLOMON'S MINES

DRAGON

JOURNEY TO THE CENTRE OF THE EARTH

PIED PIPER

TUONELA

CERBERUS

4

THE SEVEN DWARFS

PHANTOM OF THE OPERA

ALICE IN WONDER-LAND

KING ARTHUR

WITCHES

EXIT

HADES

R. STYX

BURIED HISTORY

You have reached the maze where almost everything is super-ancient. You will be history, too – if you can't find your way to the exit!

7

MODERN RUBBISH TIP

POMPEII

MAZE

MINOAN BULLS

VIKING HOARD

SUTTON HOO

ENTRANCE

AUSTRALIAN ABORIGINAL ART

BEAKER POTS

STONE AGE VILLAGE

ANCIENT WEAPONS

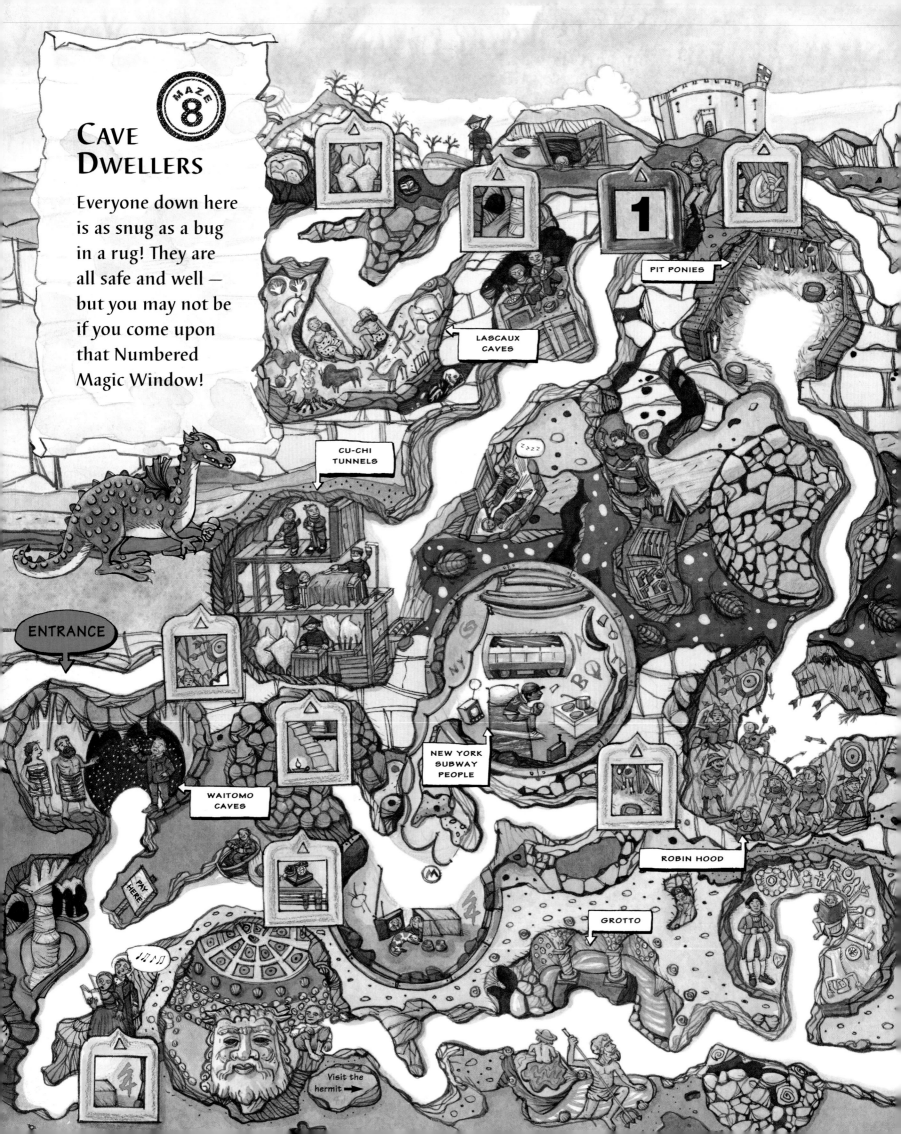

POTHOLES

CAVES OF DUNHUANG

CAPPADOCIA

PREHISTORIC CAVE DWELLINGS

SILK ROUTE

CABINET WAR ROOMS

NUCLEAR BUNKER

MODERN CAVE DWELLING

EXIT

AN ENGLISHWORM'S HOME IS HIS CAST

SMUGGLERS' CAVES

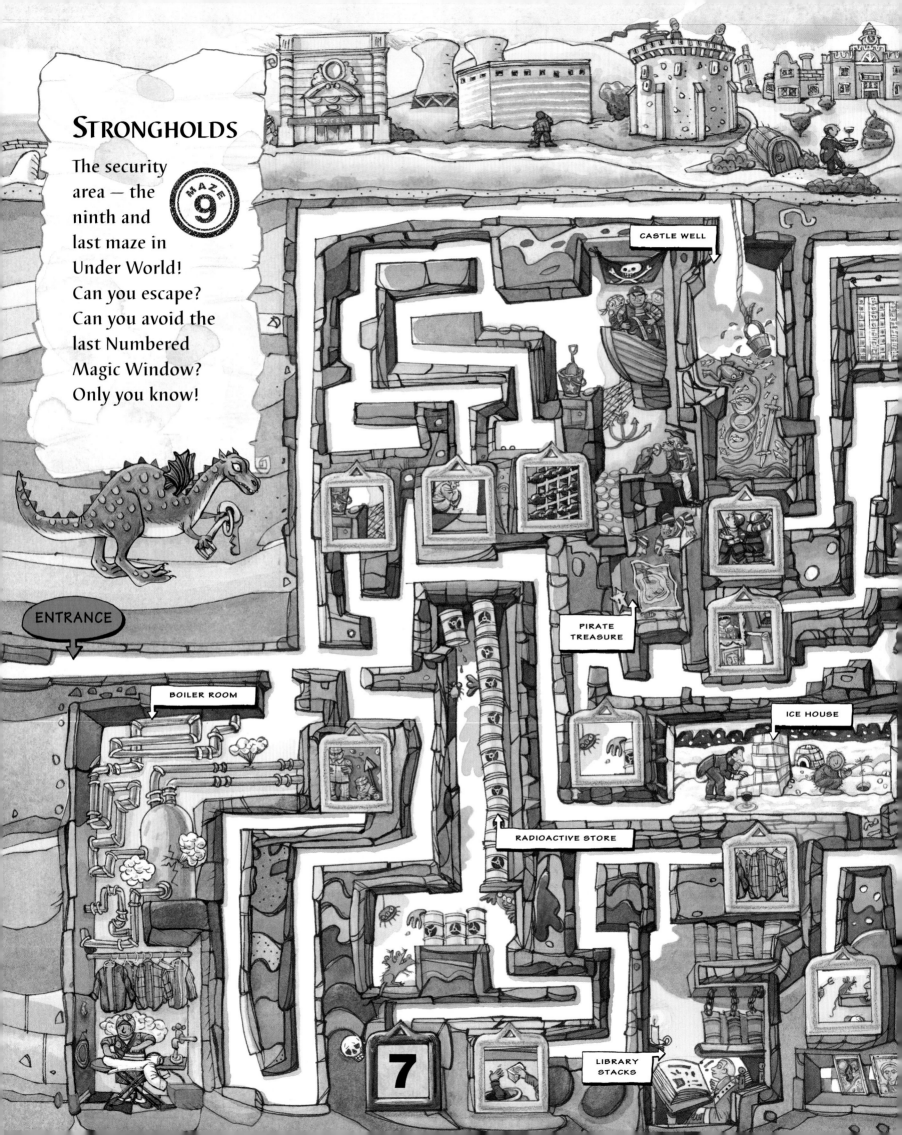

STRONGHOLDS

The security area — the ninth and last maze in Under World! Can you escape? Can you avoid the last Numbered Magic Window? Only you know!

MAZE
9

ENTRANCE

CASTLE WELL

PIRATE TREASURE

BOILER ROOM

ICE HOUSE

RADIOACTIVE STORE

7

LIBRARY STACKS

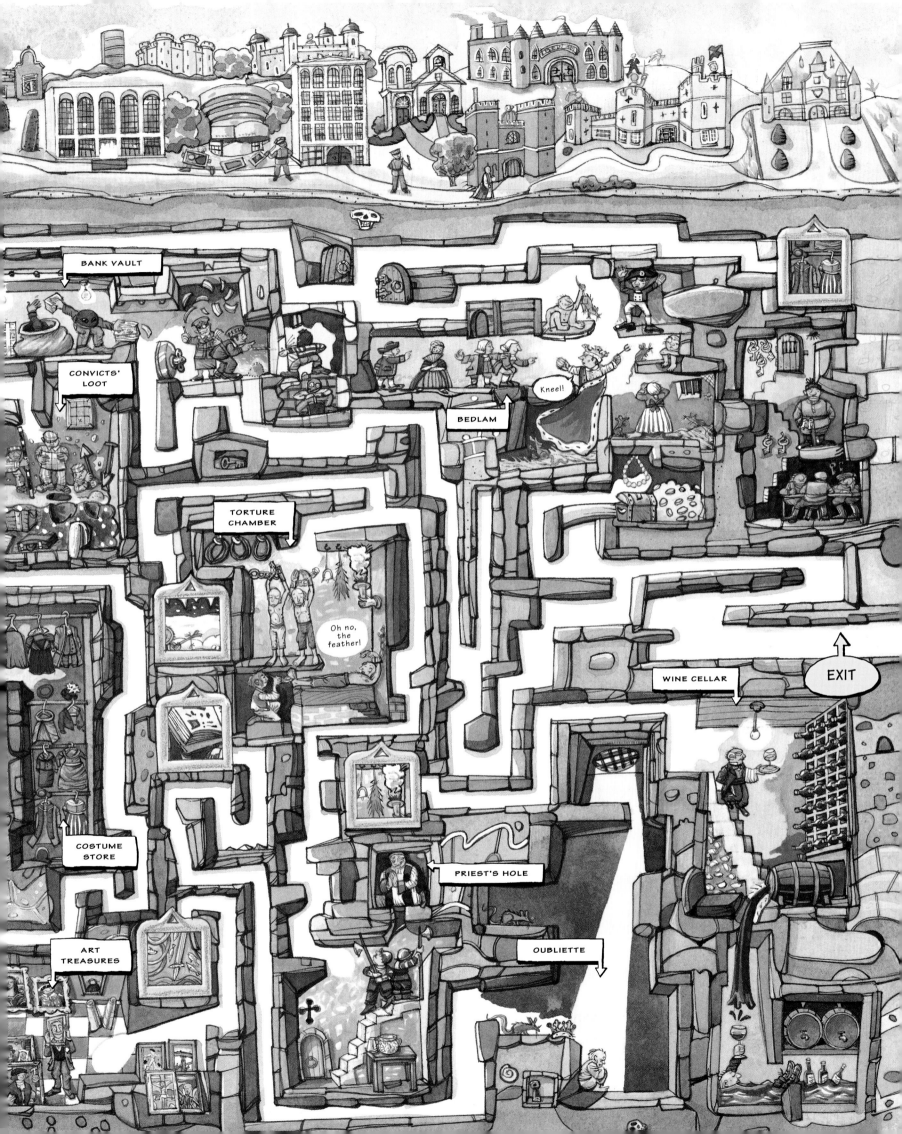

ALL ABOUT THE UNDER WORLD

MAZE 1 ~ NESTS AND BURROWS

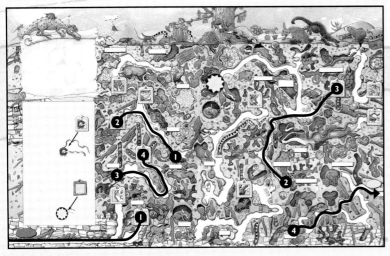

BADGERS are very house-proud. Every day they bring fresh bedding of bracken, leaves and grass into their underground set and even dig an outside loo. Badgers have strong claws for digging.

COLLARED LIZARDS were around when dinosaurs roamed the Earth. They like to sunbathe on hot stones in temperatures of up to 45°C. They live in the south-western deserts of America.

DESERT TORTOISES crawl into long tunnels to escape the heat in the dry, sandy deserts of North America.

DOGS particularly terriers and hounds, are sometimes trained to chase rabbits and foxes out of their underground homes.

DORMICE are very hard to see as they are asleep for much of the time. These animals of Eurasia and northern Africa can hibernate all winter, curled into a furry ball with their tails tucked snugly over their ears.

DUNG BEETLES roll up large balls of dung and bury them under ground with their eggs. The manure becomes a tasty snack for the young beetles when they hatch.

KANGAROO RATS live under ground in the hot deserts of Mexico and south-west America. They are champion jumpers and can leap over 2 metres into the air.

KIT FOXES run really fast in short zigzagging bursts. When they are being hunted, they may hide in the old burrows of prairie dogs. They live in the western plains and deserts of North America.

MICE inhabit all sorts of places all over the world and some of them make their homes in underground burrows. Many find their way into our houses in search of food. They are particularly fond of chocolate.

MOLES are perfect burrowing machines. They have strong legs, flat claws and a little barrel-shaped body that seems to zoom through loose soil.

OTTERS are very playful animals. They love sliding down muddy riverbanks before plunging into the water. They build dens under the roots of trees by the river, and have their families under ground.

PRAIRIE DOGS are really a kind of squirrel, but they do have a dog-like bark. They live in North America, where their underground colonies are so huge that they are called towns.

RABBITS live in a maze of underground tunnels called a warren. They are always listening out for possible dangers and shoot back into their burrows if they are afraid.

RATS are excellent burrowers, but they also live in sewers and buildings. A mother rat can produce 50 babies a year.

RATTLESNAKES are dangerous animals. They have a "rattle" of dry skin at the end of their tail which they shake before they attack.

RED FOXES live in dens and may have as many as ten hungry cubs to feed at once. Foxes eat mainly rats and voles.

WASPS sometimes build their papery nests under ground. They make the paper by chewing little bits of wood into a pulp, which they mix with saliva.

WATER VOLES are gentle, solitary animals that whistle quietly to themselves. They build underground burrows with underwater entrances to keep their babies and their food safe.

MAZE 2 ~ MINES AND QUARRIES

ARTESIAN WELLS pump up water from deep below the surface of the Earth. The name comes from Artois, in France, which has such a well. The largest artesian well, which is about 1.5 km deep, is in Australia.

COAL was originally collected from the surface. Later, people dug shafts and used rope ladders to reach coal deeper under ground.

COAL MINES are now highly mechanized, modern places, but getting the coal out of the ground is still a difficult, dangerous and expensive business.

DIAMONDS are the world's most valuable gems. They are also the hardest natural substance ever discovered and are useful for cutting and drilling other hard matter.

FOSSIL FUELS include coal, oil and gas. Three million years ago coal started out as tropical tree ferns. You can still see fossilized fern leaves in lumps of coal.

GEMSTONES are beautiful rock crystals which are rare and very precious. They only appear when molten rock cools slowly or when some minerals are heated and squeezed in the Earth's crust.

GOLD helped to make the Ancient Egyptians rich. They believed it was a gift from the Sun god and used it to decorate tombs. Modern gold mines are very hot and very deep.

GRIMES GRAVES are not graves at all, but ancient Neolithic flint mines in Norfolk, England. Miners used antlers to dig out the flints which were made into axes and knives.

INVENTIONS such as hydraulic drills and explosives have made mining more efficient. Others, such as pit props and the safety lamp, have made it less dangerous.

KING CHARLEMAGNE'S MINES were very busy. Charlemagne, or Charles the Great (724 to 814 BC), ruled most of France, Germany and northern Italy. He built many cathedrals and required a supply of brass and jewels to decorate them. He also needed metals to make coins.

KING SOLOMON'S MINES are 3000 years old. They kept 80,000 slaves busy mining the huge deposits of copper in the lands of the ancient Middle East.

METALS have been mined for thousands of years. There were copper mines in Cyprus 5000 years ago and gold mines in Peru 4000 years ago.

MINERALS are natural materials found in rocks. They include gems, fossil fuels and metals such as iron, tin, lead and copper.

MINERS today have much better equipment and work in much better conditions than in earlier times, but it is still a dangerous job.

NON-METALS include graphite, which is used in pencils, and quartz, which is used in clocks. Gypsum, a form of calcium sulphate, is used to make plaster casts.

OIL WELLS are often sunk in deserts and oceans. Engineers may have to drill 6000 metres below the sea bed to reach the spongy rock where oil is found.

SAINT BARBARA was made the miners' patron saint in medieval times. December 4th, her feast day, was celebrated with music and parades.

SALT MINES were first dug 4000 years ago in Austria. In the old Soviet Union, prisoners were sometimes sent to work in salt mines as a punishment.

STONE QUARRIES were used by the Egyptians from 3000 BC to collect limestone to build pyramids. They used the simplest of tools: stone balls, mallets and copper chisels.

THE FROZEN PRINCESS was discovered in Siberia in 1993. She died over 2200 years ago but her body, her clothes and the food buried in her grave had been deep-frozen and preserved.

GRAVE ROBBERS have stolen from graves ever since people were first buried. Tutankhamun's tomb was one of the few Egyptian sites that was not stripped of its treasure.

THE JADE PRINCESS lived in China over 2000 years ago. She had a burial suit made of 2160 pieces of jade to preserve her for the afterlife.

MAYAN TOMBS contain goods which may come in handy in the next world. Mayans often buried their dead under the floors of their houses.

MEDIEVAL TOMBS were often carved in stone and had a statue of the dead person lying on top of them. Edward, the "Black Prince", has such a tomb at Canterbury Cathedral in England.

THE MEN OF MUD are an army of model soldiers about 1.25 metres high. They were buried with a Chinese emperor 2100 years ago, to fight for him in the afterlife.

THE ROMAN CATACOMBS are underground cemeteries which date from the time of the Roman Empire. They have long tunnels and rooms cut into rock, and were used by Jewish and Christian people of the period.

ROYAL GRAVES in Ancient Greece sometimes contained treasure such as golden death masks, gold cups and bowls, tiaras and beautifully made weapons.

MAZE 3 ~ BURIAL CHAMBERS

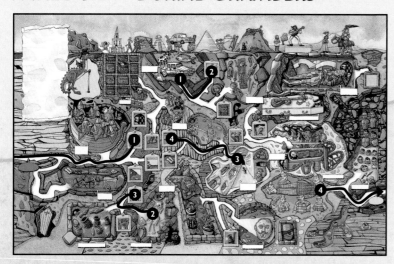

ANGLO-SAXON GRAVES were sometimes made in boats buried under a mound of soil or sand. They could contain treasure such as bronze, silver or gold.

BRONZE AGE BARROWS were usually made in pits in the ground. Sometimes they contained bronze daggers, amber and objects carved from wood or stone.

CHARIOT GRAVES are often linked with the Celts. The chariot, being a costly vehicle, was prized as a funeral offering.

CHILEAN MUMMIES are up to 7000 years old – that's 2000 years older than Egypt's. The bodies of these prehistoric people were stuffed with earth, given a wig of human hair and a painted mask.

CRYPTS are underground rooms, usually under churches. The earliest crypts were the tombs of Christian saints or martyrs.

CURIOUS COFFINS are made by wood carvers in Ghana in many different designs, to reflect a person's lifestyle. They can cost as much as the average Ghanaian earns in a whole year.

EGYPTIAN TOMBS were often hidden inside pyramids. A complex system of passages made it hard for robbers to find the treasure that was often buried with the bodies.

ELVIS PRESLEY'S GRAVE is in the grounds of Graceland, the mansion he owned in Memphis, Tennessee. The house and gardens have become a shrine for the "King of Rock and Roll".

MAZE 4 ~ TRANSPORT AND SERVICES

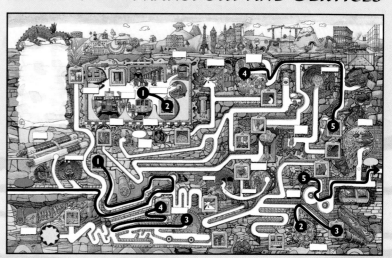

ANCIENT EGYPTIAN TUNNELLERS broke up rock by heating it to make it expand, then throwing cold water or vinegar on it. Many slaves choked and died from the fumes.

ANCIENT ROMAN TUNNELS were built to carry both vehicles and water. It took 30,000 slaves 11 years to build a tunnel to Lake Fucino, thus providing irrigation for about 20,000 hectares of farmland.

ANCIENT SUMERIAN TUNNELS built under the Euphrates River are the earliest-known tunnels, dating from 2160 BC.

CANAL TUNNELS were sometimes constructed under ground. Before motorized travel, human leg power propelled boats through the tunnels.

THE CHANNEL TUNNEL is the world's longest undersea tunnel, measuring 51.4 km. It was originally planned in 1802, but the English were afraid the French might use it as an invasion route.

DYNAMITE is often used to blow up rocks. Explosives helped to blast the world's longest road tunnel, the 15 km St Gotthard's pass near Lucerne in Switzerland.

ELECTRIC CABLES run between chambers under manholes to bring electricity to your home.

GAS PIPES carry gas from undersea gas fields over great distances to homes and industry alike. The pipes have to be very strong to prevent explosions and gas leaks which can be dangerous.

INVASION TUNNELS might have allowed the French leader Napoleon to invade Britain, but none were ever built.

IRRIGATION TUNNELS are used to carry water from rivers or reservoirs for use in farming or industry.

THE LONDON UNDERGROUND became the first-ever underground railway, when the Metropolitan line opened in 1863. The system now extends for 408 km, further than any other underground railway.

MECHANICAL MOLES are giant tunnel-boring machines. They can weigh up to 350 tonnes and make a hole 10 metres wide. Several mechanical moles were used to dig the tunnel under the English Channel.

THE MELBOURNE LOOP in Australia has just five stations. This tiny underground system lies up to 20 metres below the surface.

THE MOSCOW METRO is the world's busiest underground railway, with 3.3 billion journeys made each year. It is also one of the most beautiful with some parts resembling an underground palace.

THE NEW YORK SEWERS contain some interesting wildlife, including, according to popular belief, alligators.

THE NEW YORK SUBWAY has 469 stations, which is more than any other underground railway system.

THE PARIS METRO was first used in 1900. No point in the capital is more than 500 metres from a metro station.

ROAD TUNNELS can fill up with dangerous fumes. The Holland Tunnel under New York's Hudson River is ventilated with 400,000 cubic metres of fresh air per minute.

SEWERS are essential for taking dirty water and waste away from our homes. The Chicago TARP in America is the world's most extensive sewerage system.

TELEPHONE CABLES may each contain 5400 wires for 2700 simultaneous telephone conversations. The wires are all colour-coded to make it easier to check faults. The longest submarine cable is ANZCAN (15,151 km) which runs from Canada to Auckland and Sydney.

THE TOKYO METRO is so crowded during the rush hour that people have to be pushed on to trains.

GEOLOGISTS collect and study rocks and minerals.

GEYSERS are springs which shoot out hot water and steam.

IGNEOUS ROCKS are formed when hot liquid rock bubbles up to the surface through cracks or volcanoes.

LAVA is hot liquid rock that has burst out of the Earth's surface in volcanoes. Lava is eight times hotter than boiling water.

MAGMA is hot liquid rock under the Earth's surface. When it bubbles on to the surface it is called lava.

MAGNETISM is caused by the iron in the Earth's core, which acts like a huge rod magnet between the North and South poles.

MANGLED FOSSILS are found in metamorphic rocks. They are fossils which have been squashed out of shape by heat or pressure.

METAMORPHIC ROCKS are formed when rock is heated up or squashed so hard that it changes into something quite different – marble, for instance, which began as limestone.

MINERALS are materials that form naturally in rocks, such as salt, tin, sand and diamonds.

THE MOHO DRILL was designed to bore right down to the Earth's mantle under the Pacific Ocean, but it was not totally successful.

ROCK DATING involves measuring the decay in radioactive chemical elements. Fossil dating shows that the first, microscopic life forms began 3800 million years ago.

THE SEA FLOOR can spread when plates of rock move apart and lava flows up to the sea bed. This makes oceans expand.

SEDIMENTARY ROCKS are made of pieces of old rock and the remains of plants and animals. They are usually formed in water.

SLATE AND MARBLE are both metamorphic rocks. Slate was originally shale; marble was originally limestone.

TSUNAMIS are giant waves caused by earthquakes under the sea.

VOLCANOES are formed when hot liquid rock bursts up through the Earth's crust.

VULCANS are science fiction characters, possibly named after Vulcan, the Roman god of fire.

MAZE 5 ~ PLATES AND CRUSTS

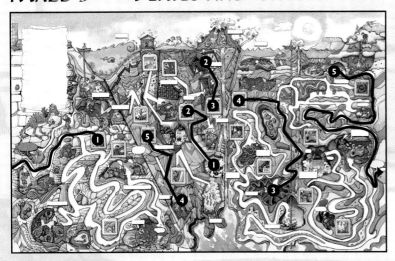

EARTH has a thin outer skin of hard rock called the crust. Below is a treacly, flexible layer called the mantle. Right in the middle is a solid core of iron and nickel.

EARTHQUAKES are caused by the movement of plates of rock in the Earth's crust and can be very destructive. People who study earthquakes are called seismologists.

FAULTS are weak lines in the Earth's crust where brittle rocks have cracked under pressure.

FOLDS in the Earth's crust are formed when huge plates of rock meet and buckle up. The European Alps and the Himalayas were formed in this way.

FOSSILS are the hardened remains of prehistoric plants and animals – skulls, bones, teeth etc. They are found in rocks.

MAZE 6 ~ MYTHS AND STORIES

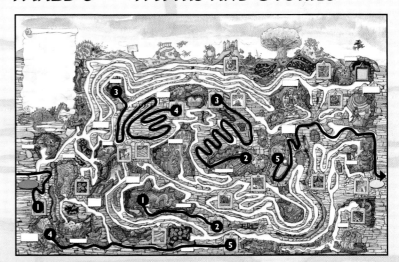

ALADDIN is a character in the ancient tales of *A Thousand and One Arabian Nights*. He is lured to a cave where he finds a magic lantern with its own genie who can grant him any wish.

ALI BABA also appears in *Arabian Nights*. He outwits the 40 thieves when he discovers their password, "Open Sesame".

ALICE IN WONDERLAND was created by Lewis Carroll in 1865. Alice falls down a rabbit hole and finds herself in a strange land where she meets the Mad Hatter, the Cheshire Cat and other curious characters.

BEOWULF is a famous Norse warrior who kills the monster Grendel. When Grendel's mother takes revenge, Beowulf follows her to her underwater cave and kills her with a magic sword.

CERBERUS is the three-headed dog who guards the entrance to Hades in Greek legends. Only the dead can pass him.

COUNT DRACULA is a 19th-century fictional character created by Bram Stoker. He is a vampire who comes out at night and drinks the blood of young women. He sleeps during the day in a coffin.

DRAGONS are found in stories from all over the world. In the Middle Ages people believed they were real and that they lived in caves.

THE GATE OF DEMONS is the doorway into the Underworld in Chinese stories.

GOBLINS are ugly underground sprites who appear in old European stories. They make mischief and play tricks on people.

HADES is the name of the Greek god of the Underworld, as well as the name of the Underworld itself.

JOURNEY TO THE CENTRE OF THE EARTH is an exciting adventure story written by Jules Verne in 1864. It was partly inspired by a French geographer who had investigated volcanoes.

KING ARTHUR and his knights lie sleeping in a cave on the island of Avalon. According to legend, Arthur may be summoned from his sleep in times of danger by the blast of a horn.

KING SOLOMON'S MINES (1885) by Rider Haggard is a story of mummies, kings and treasure. The author was inspired by the landscape, wildlife and people of Africa.

THE MINOTAUR was a man-eating monster with the head of a bull and the body of a man. It was said to live in an underground maze called the Labyrinth on the Greek island of Crete.

THE PHANTOM OF THE OPERA written in 1911, was inspired by a real-life architect who lived in the labyrinth of tunnels under the Paris Opera House.

THE PIED PIPER belongs to German folklore. He charms the rats out of Hamelin with his music. When the people fail to pay him, he charms their children into a mountain cave and they are never seen again.

THE SEVEN DWARFS are fairytale characters who dig for gold and precious stones in mountain caves.

TEUTONIC DWARFS are the legendary characters ruled by King Alberich. They made the Norse god Odin's magic sword.

TUONELA is the Finnish Underworld, an island far below the surface of the Earth. Plague, Ulcer and Gout are some of the monsters that live here.

WITCHES in old European folk tales often ride broomsticks and weave magic spells. Sometimes they live in caves.

MAZE 7 ~ BURIED HISTORY

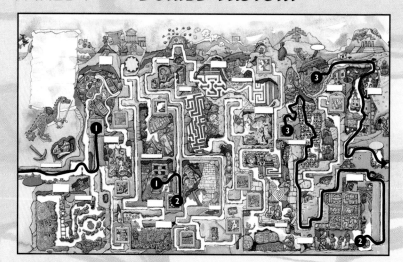

AFRICAN CAVE PAINTINGS show us that the Sahara Desert was once green and full of life; a place where people danced and animals grazed. The most famous paintings are in Tassili-n-Ajjer.

ANCIENT WEAPONS from the Middle Stone Age are smaller, and often more efficient, than earlier tools. These people of around 12,000 to 3000 BC made tiny triangular arrowheads and knives from flint.

ANUBIS the Egyptian jackal-headed god, was supposed to preside over funerals. He would weigh a person's heart to see if it was heavy with sin.

AUSTRALIAN ABORIGINAL ART is often found scratched or painted on rocks in caves. These rocks are very special to the Aborigines who regard them as a link with their ancestors.

AZTEC SKULLS from the 15th and 16th centuries remind us that these people of Central America used to sacrifice their prisoners, in the belief that human blood fed the gods and kept the sun alive.

BEAKER POTS are found in the tombs of the Beaker people who moved across Europe 4000 years ago. These people also worked with bronze and copper, and helped to rebuild Stonehenge.

CHINESE CHINA in perfect condition has been recovered from ships hundreds of years after they were wrecked on their way to Europe. Ming blue and white porcelain made in the 14th century was particulary prized.

MAYAN HIEROGLYPHS (or writing) were carved in stone at least 2000 years ago. Archaeologists study them to find out more about this mysterious Central American civilization.

MAZES are structures with many confusing passages. They date from ancient times and can be made as simple paths from hedges, solid walls or decorative materials such as mosaics. Mosaics are pictures or patterns created from tiny pieces of coloured glass and stone. Wealthy Romans liked to decorate their floors with them.

MINOAN BULLS were sacred in Crete 4000 years ago and were very popular as images for wall decorations in the King's Palace at Minos. According to legend, beneath the palace lived the man-eating Minotaur, a monster with the body of a man and the head of a bull.

MODERN RUBBISH TIPS are full of plastic. Millions and millions of tonnes of rubbish are dumped under ground every year.

POMPEII was a busy Roman city until a nearby volcano erupted and lava engulfed it. When it was discovered, 1700 years later, everything had been preserved exactly as it was in Roman times.

PUEBLO VILLAGES in the south-western states of America were built of clay. The men held meetings in underground chambers called "kivas".

STONE AGE VILLAGES were sometimes built into the ground, creating homes that were snug but rather smelly. Only the roofs were visible from above.

SUMERIAN RELICS help us to learn about one of the earliest-known civilizations, famous for inventing the wheel. Sumer was an ancient nation of Mesopotamia.

SUNKEN TREASURE is still waiting to be found in oceans all over the world. Among the richest discoveries have been Spanish galleons laden with treasure stolen from the Aztecs.

SUTTON HOO is a famous Anglo-Saxon burial site which contained the richest treasure ever unearthed in Britain. It included traces of a huge wooden boat containing a wealth of grave goods.

TROY features in many stories from Ancient Greece and the story of the Trojan Horse is especially well known. Troy was rediscovered in 1871 by the archaeologist Heinrich Schliemann.

VIKING HOARDS may contain coins, carvings, swords and even fish bones. The Vikings were sea pirates and adventurers of the 8th to the 10th century, and these artefacts tell us something about their life.

WALL PAINTINGS were popular in many cultures. The Ancient Chinese liked geometric patterns and floral designs, which often looked three-dimensional.

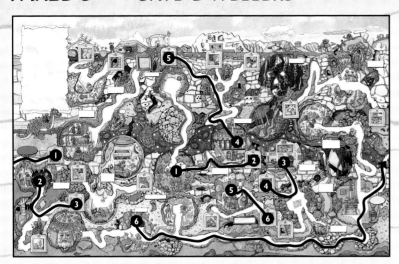

CABINET WAR ROOMS (or bunkers) in London, have been kept just as they were during the Second World War when Winston Churchill used them.

CAPPADOCIA is a famous collection of underground villages in Turkey. It is built out of a natural landscape which was formed thousands of years ago by volcanoes and earthquakes. Early Christians lived here and because they were afraid of persecution they built their towns under ground, complete with homes, chapels decorated with wall paintings, wineries, cemeteries and even prisons – all on several levels.

THE CAVES OF DUNHUANG are an amazing network of about 500 grottoes in China. They lie on the old Silk Road, the ancient trade route between East and West. The caves contain murals which show 1000 years of early Chinese and Tibetan life.

THE CU-CHI TUNNELS in southern Vietnam date from the Vietnam War. In the 1960s there were over 250 km of tunnels, in many places several storeys deep. They housed hospitals, weapons factories, kitchens, command centres and air-raid shelters. There were concealed trapdoor entrances to the tunnels to keep them secret from the enemy.

GROTTOES are usually artificial caves with mysterious dark passages and hidden entrances. They are often elaborately decorated with shells.

THE LASCAUX CAVES are covered with beautiful prehistoric paintings, mainly hunting scenes featuring bison, horses and deer. They were painted around 20,000 BC but have survived because the caves in this part of France are so dry.

MODERN CAVE DWELLINGS are still found in many parts of the world. In Coober Pedy, Australia, people live under ground to escape the heat of the desert, which can soar to well over 40°C.

NEW YORK SUBWAY PEOPLE are homeless. Many of them sleep on benches, but some make real homes for themselves in the numerous disused tunnels.

NUCLEAR BUNKERS have been built all over the world. They were designed to protect people from nuclear attack. In China, some nuclear bunkers have been converted into hotels.

PIT PONIES worked in mines; they were used to haul coal in waggons under ground.

POTHOLES are different from caves because they are vertical rather than horizontal. Exploring these underground shafts and tunnels has developed into a sport called potholing, requiring special clothing and safety equipment.

PREHISTORIC CAVE DWELLINGS provided shelter from rain, wind and snow as well as safety from wild animals.

ROBIN HOOD was said to have lived near the town of Nottingham, in England. Underneath Nottingham Castle there is a maze of sandstone tunnels and passages, which you can still visit today.

SMUGGLERS' CAVES were usually used to hide contraband.

THE WAITOMO CAVES in New Zealand have been carved out of limestone by rivers and streams. They are famous because they are full of glow-worms. They also have huge chambers of stalagmites and stalactites.

ART TREASURES are sometimes buried under ground to protect them when a foreign army invades. During the Second World War several countries safeguarded their masterpieces by hiding them away.

BANK VAULTS are often set deep under ground, behind strong steel doors. Complicated locks and hi-tech security systems help to ensure that money and valuables can be safely stored.

BEDLAM was London's first "lunatic asylum". It was founded as a priory in the 13th century and became notorious for the terrible conditions in which mentally ill patients had to live. The word "bedlam" is now used to mean an uproar.

BOILER ROOMS are hot, smelly places that house heating systems for hotels and other large buildings.

CASTLE WELLS were essential, especially if the people inside the castle were being attacked. As long as they had a safe supply of water, they could survive a protracted siege.

CONVICTS' LOOT has to be hidden quickly. The loot from England's Great Train Robbery in 1963 has never been found.

COSTUME STORES can contain hundreds of different outfits, which need to be kept safe and dry. Many big modern theatres have an underground store which can be reached by lift. That way the costumes are always near at hand.

ICE HOUSES were used to keep food cool in the days before fridges. They were found only in the grounds of castles or big wealthy houses. A pit about 7 metres deep was lined with stone or brick. Ice stacked between layers of straw remained solid for up to three years.

LIBRARY STACKS are shelves of books, all waiting to be borrowed. The British Library stores 12 million books in four huge basements. At 23 metres, they are the deepest in London.

OUBLIETTES were dungeons entered from above via a trapdoor. Here prisoners were kept for a very long time, often secretly until forgotten. The name comes from the French word *oublier* meaning "to forget".

PIRATE TREASURE from centuries ago may still be lying in underground hiding places. Edward Teach (later called "Blackbeard") and Captain Kidd were famous pirates who started their careers as law-abiding sailors. They were both captured and killed, but much of their treasure was never found.

A PRIEST'S HOLE was a tiny, secret hiding place built into houses from the time of Elizabeth I until the end of the 17th century. In those days, Catholics were very unpopular and priests had to hide for their safety.

RADIOACTIVE STORES contain the waste that is left from nuclear power stations. It is very dangerous to all life and can take 100,000 years to decay, which is why it is buried deep under ground.

TORTURE CHAMBERS have been used throughout history by governments, powerful people and criminals to make their prisoners confess to things they have done, or to reveal information. Even today, torture is still practised in some parts of the world.

WINE CELLARS are usually under ground where it is dark and cool. Many wines improve in flavour when stored in wooden barrels.

First published 1999 by Walker Books Ltd
87 Vauxhall Walk, London SE 11 5HJ

2 4 6 8 10 9 7 5 3 1

© 1999 Gillian Clements

This book has been typeset in Barbedor.

Printed in Hong Kong

British Library Cataloguing in Publication Data
A catalogue record for this book is available
from the British Library.

ISBN 0-7445-4441-6